CLOZE CLUES

Written by Dorothy Probert
Illustrated by Beverly Armstrong

The Learning Works

Edited by Sherri M. Butterfield

The purchase of this book entitles the individual teacher to reproduce copies for use in the classroom.

The reproduction of any part for an entire school or school system or for commercial use is strictly prohibited.

No form of this work may be reproduced or transmitted or recorded without written permission from the publisher.

Contents

What Is Cloze?

The term **cloze** is derived from the concept of closure. In this context, **closure** is the process of making a connection between two ideas or of completing a thought. When a text passage is prepared in cloze format, some words are omitted. Spaces or lines are inserted to indicate where these words have been left out. The reader must use the meaning and structure of the remaining text to determine which word could be used to fill each space and restore meaning to the entire passage.

In standard cloze format, every *n*th word is omitted in a regular pattern from a passage of continuous, meaningful text. Typically, every fifth, eighth, or eleventh word is left out. This rather rigid format is used in cloze materials written for testing purposes. In this format, only the exact word used in the original text is accepted as correct.

For instructional purposes, the standard cloze format is usually modified. The formats for modified cloze passages are almost endless. The behavioral purpose determines what kinds of reading materials are used, where and how frequently words are omitted, and what kinds of clues are provided for the reader. In the modified format, any word that is syntactically correct and does not alter the author's meaning is accepted as correct.

Modified cloze formats permit the use of many different exercise designs, including multiple choice, word list clue, graphic clue, and word length clue. The multiple choice design is used in most standardized tests and for many workbooks.

a. but also
b. *whereas*
c. even
d. rather than

To the Teacher

The exercises in this book are designed to teach recognition and use of clue words to bring understanding to the reading process. They will help students increase their comprehension of reading texts and improve their scores on the comprehension sections of reading tests. Because these exercises are intended to improve reading power, not reading speed, they are untimed. For convenience, they have been organized into four sets of practices that rely primarily on either noun substitute clues, transforming word clues, time and sequence word clues, or summary word clues.

The modified cloze format and multiple choice design have been used to prepare these exercises. For each numbered blank within a reading passage, there is a list of four possible word responses. Only one of these word responses is semantically and syntactically correct. Through classroom discussion of sentence and passage clues, students are encouraged to recognize and choose this one correct word. Once students are familiar with the cloze format and procedure, they should be able to complete each exercise with 75 percent accuracy.

Introducing Students to the Cloze Process

1. Explain to students the reasons for using cloze passages as skill-building exercises and the instructions for completing them.

2. Select a passage and omit certain words from it.

3. Discuss with students your reasons for choosing this particular passage and point out its relevance to curriculum, current events, or season.

4. Ask students to read the passage silently.

5. Read the passage aloud, sentence by sentence, or ask a student to do so.

6. As the passage is read, have students suggest words that might be written on the numbered lines. If students have difficulty thinking of words to suggest, point out the clues that appear before and after each line, as well as the clues that occur elsewhere in the passage.

7. Accept as correct all semantically and syntactically appropriate responses, but ask students to give reasons for the words they suggest.

8. Use the resulting discussion to encourage an understanding of the structure of the English language and to help students determine acceptable responses and eliminate unacceptable ones.

9. Compare the completed cloze passage, into which words suggested by students have now been inserted, with the original passage. In what ways are they the same? In what ways are they different?

10. Discuss the ways in which the meaning of a particular sentence or of the overall passage may be altered by the acceptance and insertion of certain word responses that differ from those used in the original passage by its author.

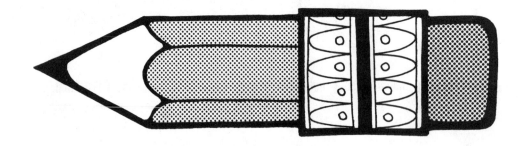

Instructions for Teachers

1. Before using each exercise, review with class members the Instructions for Students on page 8.

2. Read with class members the instructions that appear in the box at the top of the particular exercise they will be doing.

3. Allow students plenty of time to complete the exercise and insist that they do so without help of any kind.

4. Once students have completed the exercise, use the Answer Key on pages 47–48 to check their answers. Accept as correct only those answers that are listed in the key.

5. Count the number of correct answers and enter this number on the line provided at the bottom of the exercise.

6. Enter the number of correct answers in the box provided on the Score Chart on page 45.

7. Using the Table of Percentages on page 46, determine what percentage of the total number of answers is represented by the number of correct answers.

8. Enter this percent score in the box provided on page 45.

9. If a student scores below 75 percent on any exercise, determine what concept is causing the student to have difficulty, reteach this concept, and then assign the next exercise.

Instructions for Students

The cloze exercises in this book are designed to help you become a better reader. To do them effectively, follow these instructions carefully so that each passage you complete makes sense.

1. Read the *first* and *last* sentence in a cloze passage to determine what the passage is about.

2. Read the entire passage. A numbered line indicates that a word or phrase has been left out. Ignore these numbered lines and keep reading. *Read the entire passage before you choose a word or phrase for any numbered line.*

3. When you have finished reading, look again at the entire passage. Locate clues that will help you supply the missing words. Remember that the clues you need may come before or after the numbered lines in the passage.

4. Supply the missing word or words for each numbered line by underlining one of the lettered choices listed for that number in the column on the right. You may choose any word or phrase that allows the sentence to make sense and conveys the author's meaning.

5. Reread the entire passage, substituting your word choices for the numbered lines.

6. Does the passage make sense now? If not, look back at the words you chose and change the ones that do not seem to fit.

7. Now reread the entire passage. Are you satisfied? If so, prepare to check your answers. If not, try changing another word or two, and then read the passage again.

Noun Substitute Clues

A **noun** is a word that names a person, place, thing, or idea. If the same name for a person, place, thing, or idea is used over and over in a written passage, it becomes repetitious and boring; therefore, creative authors often use substitutes for these names.

Sometimes a writer uses a **pronoun**. The pronouns that are used in place of **people names** are

I	me	myself	my, mine
you	him	himself	your(s)
he	her	herself	his
she	us	yourself	hers
it	them	yourselves	its
we	one	themselves	ours
they			their(s)

The pronouns that are sometimes substituted for **place names** are

it	they
its	them
	their(s)

The pronouns that are used in place of **thing or idea names** are

it	they
one	them
	their(s)

Sometimes, a writer substitutes one noun for another. Look at the example below.

> I live in a large white <u>house</u>.
> My <u>home</u> is on a high hill.

In this example, the word <u>home</u> has been substituted for the word <u>house</u>. Both words are nouns, but the use of two different nouns varies the word content of these sentences and makes them more interesting to read. Now look at this example.

> My <u>mother and father</u> take good care of me.
> My <u>parents</u> think that I am special.

In this example, the word <u>parents</u> has been substituted for the words <u>mother and father</u>. Here, one word takes the place of three.

Left margin: us · its · himself · you · I · myself · it · she

Right margin: mine · yourself · them · him · ours · their

Interesting Animals That Live Around Us

Follow the instructions on page 8. For each numbered line in the passage, choose one of the lettered words on the right. Underline the word you choose.

If you look around you, you will discover that the world is full of interesting creatures. For example, the monarch butterfly is interesting because, although it appears to be very delicate, it is strong enough to migrate in large swarms over great distances.

Another interesting animal is the zebra-tailed lizard. This tiny __1__ got its name from the stripes on its tail. Zebra-tailed lizards are among the fastest reptiles. They run on their strong hind legs, without using their forelimbs and with their tails curled forward for balance. They have been clocked at speeds up to eighteen miles per hour.

Unlike some other animals, the house mouse is not helpful to man. This __2__ is found almost everywhere—in all kinds of buildings, as well as in fields and pastures. It frequently invades food supplies and can cause disease.

Pocket gophers are also very destructive rodents. With __3__ sharp, chisel-like teeth, they are capable of destroying the vegetation on both lawns and pasturelands. They even burrow beneath gardens and pull plants down by the roots. Occasionally, a carrot or radish will disappear into the ground as the startled gardener watches.

The barn owl is helpful. Because of the distinctive outline on its face, it is also called the monkey-faced owl. Barn owls prey upon the house mouse and other small rodents. Even though these __4__ are fairly common, you may never see one. They do most of their hunting at night.

(Exercise 1 is continued on page 11.)

1. a. monarch
   b. lizard
   c. friend
   d. pet

2. a. helper
   b. pet
   c. rodent
   d. lizard

3. a. rodent
   b. these
   c. large
   d. their

4. a. faces
   b. animals
   c. birds
   d. things

Interesting Animals That Live Around Us
(continued)

The barn swallow lives along the Pacific Coast. This __5__ is often seen skimming over grass-covered hills and meadows. Barn swallows build their half-saucer-shaped nests on the rafters of barns and under culverts and bridges. These birds make their nests of mud and grass, and line them with feathers. Barn swallows are helpful to us because they spend most of the daylight hours in the air searching for flying insects, which are the main part of their diet.

The common toad is a valuable asset in any garden. Its remarkable tongue is a most efficient tool for catching the enormous number of insects __6__ requires daily. When not in use, this tongue remains coiled like a spring inside the toad's mouth. With lightning speed, this amphibian can shoot out its tongue toward unwary insects that wander within its range.

Ladybird beetles are sometimes called ladybugs, but they are not "bugs" at all. They are insects and are members of the beetle family. __7__ food is primarily plant lice and scale insects. Orange growers turn these __8__ loose in their groves to control pests that might otherwise destroy their trees and fruit. Many children like to play with ladybirds, and a nursery rhyme has been written about them.

5. a. bug
b. creature
c. bird
d. animal

6. a. this
b. it
c. they
d. frogs

7. a. Their
b. This
c. Animal
d. Bird

8. a. birds
b. pests
c. beetles
d. lice

Number of correct answers _____

Name _____

How Living Things Swim

Follow the instructions on page 8. For each numbered line in the passage, choose one of the lettered words on the right. Underline the word you choose.

Different kinds of creatures swim in different ways. Penguins, for example, swim with their wings. Though the wings of these __1__ work well underwater, they are too narrow to support the birds in the air and cannot be used for flying. The penguin is the only bird that uses its wings to fly through the water.

Shrimps, lobsters, and their relatives swim backward. They move by flicking their fanlike tails. When these tails are jerked forward, __2__ push against the water and drive the creatures backward. In addition to their tails, shrimps also have little paddles on their sides, which enable them to swim forward.

Squids also swim backward, but in another way. __3__ draw in water and then squirt it out through a tube under __4__ large, goggle-like eyes. Squids are actually jet-propelled. They can swim much faster than fish of the same size. They are sometimes called "sea arrows" because of their shape and speed.

A jellyfish is not a true fish because it does not have a backbone. This __5__ swims near the surface of the water by alternately spreading and closing __6__ soft, umbrella-shaped body. As the jellyfish moves silently through the water, its slender tentacles and lacy streamers trail behind.

(Exercise 2 is continued on page 13.)

1. a. oars
   b. amphibians
   c. creatures
   d. bodies

2. a. he
   b. they
   c. this
   d. that

3. a. Fish
   b. Fins
   c. They
   d. Shrimps

4. a. its
   b. those
   c. their
   d. the

5. a. fish
   b. thing
   c. body
   d. creature

6. a. them
   b. parts
   c. its
   d. that

How Living Things Swim
(continued)

We often say that fish swim with their fins, but this is not true. A fish swims by moving __7__ body from side to side, thus pushing __8__ through the water. Fins help the fish to remain upright and enable it to change direction.

The otter is swift and graceful on land, and __9__ is equally adept in water. This fur-bearing mammal swims with __10__ four webbed feet and uses its tail to steer and balance itself. In the water, an otter can twist and turn as easily as any fish.

Seals hobble or wriggle clumsily on land. __11__ real home is in seawater. Their smooth, torpedo-shaped bodies are just right for speedy swimming. Their hind legs extend backward in a way that resembles the tail fins of fish.

Ducks, gulls, and many other birds swim with their broad, webbed feet, instead of with wings like penguins. These __12__ are skilled swimmers and can glide quickly across a lake. When these birds are alarmed, they flap their wings and fly away.

7. a. this
   b. its
   c. a
   d. their

8. a. them
   b. this
   c. it
   d. itself

9. a. it
   b. them
   c. to
   d. otters

10. a. the
    b. all
    c. its
    d. these

11. a. This
    b. The
    c. Its
    d. Their

12. a. animals
    b. gulls
    c. ducks
    d. creatures

Number of correct answers _____

Name _____

Smokey Bear, the Famous Forest Ranger

Follow the instructions on page 8. For each numbered line in the passage, choose one of the lettered words on the right. Underline the word you choose.

One bright morning, a small bear cub was following his mother through the sunshine in a pine-scented New Mexico mountain forest. Suddenly, __1__ mother stopped, sniffed the air, and began to flee with all of the other forest creatures.

Left behind, the puzzled little cub watched as choking smoke and searing flames came nearer to __2__. Finally, not knowing what else to do, he climbed a pine tree and remained there while the forest fire roared and crackled below him. The flames licked at __3__ shaggy fur and singed his tender paws. The little cub was very frightened.

After the fire had passed through the forest, a ranger went out to check the damage. __4__ was surprised to find a bear cub clinging to the top of a burned pine tree. The ranger rescued the __5__ and took him to the game warden's home. There, the warden and the rangers cared for the cub while he recovered from his ordeal.

The forest rangers decided it would be a very good idea to use the cub to teach American children to be more careful with fire. The __6__ was put on a plane and sent to the National Zoo in Washington, D.C., where he lived for many years. This bear became known to children all over America as Smokey Bear.

(Exercise 3 is continued on page 15.)

1. a. their
   b. bears
   c. his
   d. my

2. a. it
   b. others
   c. him
   d. trees

3. a. this
   b. little
   c. their
   d. his

4. a. It
   b. He
   c. Ranger
   d. Then

5. a. forest
   b. tree
   c. cub
   d. damage

6. a. ranger
   b. bear
   c. fire
   d. forest

Name _____

Smokey Bear, the Famous Forest Ranger
(continued)

One of the lessons Smokey Bear taught is *not* to play with matches. One tiny match lighted in your home could cause a giant fire that would burn down your entire __7__. Before you throw away a match that has been struck, break __8__ in two and feel the burned end to be certain that it is no longer hot.

Another lesson that Smokey Bear taught is to be careful with campfires. Build your fire on well-cleared ground, away from trees and bushes, where __9__ cannot spread. If possible, place a ring of stones around it. Before you leave your campsite, pour water on your fire until you have drowned each tiny spark.

A frequent cause of forest fires is lighted cigarettes that are tossed carelessly through car windows. Although children do not smoke, Smokey Bear wanted __10__ to help him teach their parents to crush out their cigarettes in the car ashtray. If __11__ smoke outside the car, they should be cautioned to crush out __12__ cigarettes in safe places. If your parents smoke, remind them that a tiny spark left in a cigarette can grow into a giant fire that will burn an entire forest and destroy the homes of many animals like Smokey.

Help Smokey Bear prevent forest fires by being careful about the way you handle and use anything that burns and by reminding your parents and friends to do the same.

7. a. match
   b. forest
   c. room
   d. house

8. a. them
   b. it
   c. he
   d. camp

9. a. they
   b. you
   c. it
   d. its

10. a. people
    b. bears
    c. them
    d. parents

11. a. children
    b. adults
    c. bears
    d. cigarettes

12. a. his
    b. their
    c. those
    d. this

Number of correct answers _____

Name _____

A Different Kind of Home

Follow the instructions on page 8. For each numbered line in the passage, choose one of the lettered words on the right. Underline the word you choose.

When people think of a home, they think of a building made of wood, brick, or stone. Some creatures live in buildings made of these materials, but there are other creatures that live in the grass and underground.

One creature that lives in grass is the froghopper. Also called the spittlebug, this drab-colored __1__ has a "froggy" look when it is at rest on a leaf or plant stem. Female froghoppers deposit a sticky juice on the stems or leaves of grasses to protect __2__ eggs. Young froghoppers, which are called nymphs, continue covering themselves with this bubbly juice while they feed. Ordinarily, tiny froghopper nymphs are completely hidden by the unique houses of froth they build in this way.

Grass is the home of another hopper, the grasshopper. This __3__ does not build any house at all. Instead, it keeps busy hopping through the grass and onto plants. With its long, strong hind legs, the grasshopper can jump many times its own length. With its broad wings, it can extend these jumps by gliding. Grasshoppers have enormous appetites. Because they eat __4__ weight in leaves each day, a swarm of them can quickly lay waste the grass on a lawn or the grain in a field.

1. a. mammal
   b. amphibian
   c. insect
   d. frog

2. a. her
   b. their
   c. large
   d. its

3. a. reptile
   b. animal
   c. insect
   d. mammal

4. a. its
   b. his
   c. heavy
   d. their

(Exercise 4 is continued on page 17.)

Name _____

A Different Kind of Home
(continued)

One of the noisiest insects in the grass is the common field cricket. You hear this __5__ chirping merrily before you see it. The cricket is a musician, not a singer. It has no voice. It "chirps" by vibrating its wings together. Crickets hear with organs located on __6__ forelegs. They are not picky eaters and will feed on almost anything—plants, other insects, or even scraps left by careless picnickers.

Earthworms make their home beneath the grass, in the ground. These __7__ live in tunnels during the day. Usually, they come out only at night; but if there is a heavy rain, earthworms come out during the day. When their tunnels fill with water, these __8__ come out so that they will not drown. Earthworms are very beneficial because the tunnels they dig allow water and air to seep into the soil.

Ants are some of the most interesting creatures that live underground. They build cities in the soil. In an ant city, there are special places where eggs are laid, where young ants are raised, where food is stored, and where garbage is dumped. Each ant community has a queen that does nothing but lay eggs. Workers in the ant community look after __9__. These workers also take care of the eggs, gather food, feed the __10__, and keep their __11__ clean. Some ants keep "cows." __12__ cows are really aphids, tiny insects that suck juice from the stems and leaves of plants. The aphids turn this juice into a sticky substance called honeydew. Using their antennae, the ants stroke, or "milk," the aphids to get some of this honeydew.

The grass and ground are home to many interesting and unusual creatures.

5. a. singer
   b. animal
   c. pest
   d. grass-
      dweller

6. a. those
   b. his
   c. its
   d. their

7. a. reptiles
   b. bugs
   c. creatures
   d. insects

8. a. worms
   b. insects
   c. rodents
   d. bugs

9. a. her
   b. it
   c. this
   d. them

10. a. ants
    b. young
    c. children
    d. themselves

11. a. place
    b. village
    c. city
    d. babies

12. a. His
    b. These
    c. Dairy
    d. Milk

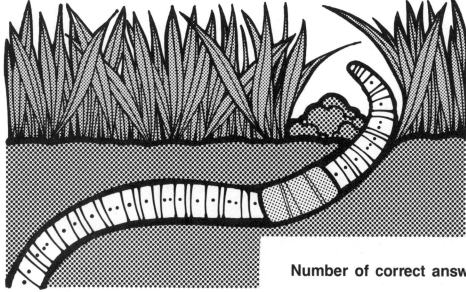

Number of correct answers _____

Central America

Follow the instructions on page 8. For each numbered line in the passage, choose one of the lettered words on the right. Underline the word you choose.

Central America is a group of seven small countries crowded together on a land bridge that connects North and South America. These countries are Belize, Costa Rica, El Salvador, Guatemala, Honduras, Nicaragua, and Panama. Because these __1__ lie near the equator, their climate is tropical, and their weather is warm and humid.

The first people to live in Central America probably came from Asia. Thousands of years ago, __2__ crossed the land bridge that once connected Russia with Alaska. Over many generations, these people slowly migrated south through Canada, the Pacific Northwest, California, the Southwest, and Mexico. Finally, they settled in the area we now know as the Yucatan Peninsula and Central America.

Once they reached this __3__, they stopped wandering. They gathered together in small groups and began to grow plants for food. As these __4__ became larger, they built roads and temples and cities. Within these cities, they developed their own, very special, way of life.

People living in Europe first heard about Central America when Christopher Columbus returned from his fourth and final voyage. In 1502, this Italian __5__ discovered Honduras while searching for the riches of the Indies. Columbus admired the gold jewelry the Central American __6__ wore. __7__ tried to persuade them to lead him to their __8__. When they refused, Columbus returned to Spain believing that he had failed to find the Old World riches he sought and not realizing that, in finding Central America, he had discovered another part of the New World.

1. a. country
   b. nations
   c. land
   d. people

2. a. they
   b. them
   c. countries
   d. nations

3. a. bridge
   b. city
   c. area
   d. country

4. a. people
   b. bridges
   c. plants
   d. groups

5. a. ship
   b. temple
   c. explorer
   d. sailors

6. a. natives
   b. cities
   c. they
   d. sailors

7. a. They
   b. He
   c. Sailors
   d. Explorer

8. a. rich
   b. city
   c. temple
   d. treasure

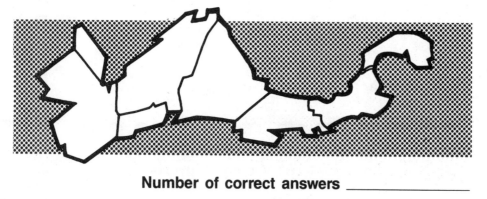

Number of correct answers _____

Transforming Word Clues

The English word **transform** comes from the Latin words *trans*, meaning "across, beyond, over, through, or to the other side of," and *forma*, meaning "form, figure, or shape." In Latin, these two words are combined in the verb *transformare*, meaning "to change." Thus, the English word **transform** means "to change in appearance, form, shape, or structure."

Transforming words are words that change the shape of an idea, modify the meaning of a sentence, or show the way in which people, places, things, or ideas differ. For example, to show the way in which two places differ, an author might write the following sentence:

Outside, the wind howled, and the snow swirled;
<u>but</u> inside, the fire was cozy and warm.

In this sentence, the transforming word <u>but</u> warns the reader that the writer is comparing two places—the outside and the inside—and is pointing out a difference between them.

Consider the sentence

Every bone in Jim's body ached; <u>nevertheless</u>, he struggled valiantly on.

In this sentence, you might have expected the author to write

Every bone in Jim's body ached, so he decided to stop and rest.

A clever author uses transforming words to warn the reader to expect the unexpected. In this example, the transforming word <u>nevertheless</u> warns you to expect Jim to go on rather than to stop.

Watch for these transforming words and phrases as you read.

although	instead of	rather than
but	nevertheless	therefore
but also	not only	whereas
even though	on the other hand	yet
however		

Notice where authors use these words and phrases and how they clarify the relationships between ideas, underscore contrasts or differences, and change the meanings of sentences or passages.

TRANSFORMING

Sleepwalking

> Follow the instructions on page 8. For each numbered line in the passage, choose one of the lettered words or phrases on the right. Underline the word or phrase you choose.

Some people walk in their sleep. The things people do while they are sleepwalking can be funny; ___1___, they can also be dangerous. For example, in one amazing incident, an eleven-year-old boy walked in his sleep one night and was found the next morning nearly one hundred miles from his home. The police who discovered him were somewhat amused, ___2___ they did not think it a laughing matter when they discovered that the boy had hopped a freight train while he was asleep!

Another sleepwalker's experience was quite different ___3___ equally dangerous. This sleepwalker was a man whose second-floor bedroom opened onto a balcony. Because this man was aware that he frequently walked in his sleep, he had a very secure lock placed on the door that led from his bedroom to the balcony. The locksmith who installed the lock told the sleepwalker that it would be impossible for him to unlock the door in his sleep. ___4___, the man did walk out onto the balcony while he was asleep, climb over the railing, and fall twenty feet to the ground below, fracturing his spine.

1. a. and
b. thus
c. however
d. then

2. a. but
b. thus
c. and
d. therefore

3. a. instead
b. but
c. and
d. thus

4. a. Even though
b. And
c. Nevertheless
d. Also

(Exercise 6 is continued on page 21.)

Sleepwalking
(continued)

There is a story about another man who placed a foolproof lock on a sliding glass door which he frequently unlocked while he was sleepwalking. The lock did prevent the man from unlocking the door in his sleep, ___5___ he sleepwalked right through the glass. He awoke outside with blood spurting from his wrist. ___6___ protecting the man by preventing him from going outside in his sleep, the lock had caused him to suffer a serious injury.

It is true that sleepwalkers do amusing things during their walks; ___7___, these humorous incidents can result in serious injury. It is fortunate that only a small number of people walk while they are asleep.

5. a. instead
b. or
c. and
d. but

6. a. Rather than
b. Even though
c. And
d. But

7. a. instead
b. and
c. rather
d. however

Number of correct answers _____

Changing Times

Follow the instructions on page 8. For each numbered line in the passage, choose one of the lettered words or phrases on the right. Underline the word or phrase you choose.

When your grandparents were young, society had very different ideas about the roles men and women were expected to play. Since that time, the proper roles of the sexes have been redefined; ___1___, many questions about these roles remain unanswered.

The old attitudes were evident in the play of children. Thirty years ago, young girls were encouraged to play with dolls and have tea parties; ___2___ young boys were expected to play with guns and to participate in games that required athletic skill.

These differences in toys and games were reflections of the differences in the roles males and females were expected to assume in adult life. ___3___ some girls went to college, all young women were expected to marry and become homemakers. Likewise, all young men were expected to learn a trade or to prepare for a profession that would enable them to become providers.

The old attitudes toward roles were apparent in the schools. On the one hand, girls were required to take courses in cooking and sewing. ___4___, boys were required to take courses in math, science, and woodworking. At this time, many educators believed that girls lacked the mental discipline needed to master mathematics and the sciences.

When women found it necessary to enter the work force because of a husband's illness or death, they had to take low-paying jobs as clerks, housekeepers, seamstresses, or secretaries and were not allowed to become doctors, lawyers, and professors. Women who did find their way into the professional ranks were paid lower wages than men ___5___ they worked as hard, as long, and as well.

Ideas about the types of work women are capable of doing and about how they should be paid for their time have changed, ___6___ there are still some areas in which society treats women as its second-class citizens.

1. a. although
   b. whereas
   c. however
   d. and

2. a. though
   b. whereas
   c. even
   d. rather than

3. a. Although
   b. But
   c. However
   d. Instead of

4. a. But
   b. On the other hand
   c. Rather
   d. Instead of

5. a. instead of
   b. but
   c. yet
   d. even though

6. a. because
   b. whereas
   c. but
   d. since

Number of correct answers _____

Name _____

Acquiring Knowledge

> Follow the instructions on page 8. For each numbered line in the passage, choose one of the lettered words or phrases on the right. Underline the word or phrase you choose.

Much of the knowledge children acquire is taught to them by their parents. From their parents, children learn the speech patterns and the social customs of the society in which they live. Also from their parents, children acquire attitudes and values. __1__ many generations of parents have carefully taught their ideas to many generations of children, this knowledge has not been passed down exactly as it was received. __2__, as the children have grown up, they have evaluated the old wisdom, deciding how much of it to keep and pass on to future generations, and how much to discard and replace with new ideas.

Many centuries ago, parents were probably able to teach a child all he needed to know to survive. They could show him how to find or build a shelter, how to catch or grow food, and how to make and use tools or weapons. Life has become much more complex, __3__ basic survival skills are no longer enough. Today, children need to develop a broader base of knowledge and a wider range of skills. For this reason, no one information source is sufficient. Children must learn not only from many different teachers __4__ from a wide variety of information sources as well.

One commonly used source of information is books. __5__ books are usually a reliable source of information, not all of them are accurate. To evaluate the accuracy of a book, you need to know when the book was written and by whom. You want up-to-date information written by knowledgeable authors who have not allowed their personal opinions to taint the truth of their texts.

1. a. However
   b. Although
   c. And
   d. But

2. a. And
   b. But
   c. Although
   d. Instead

3. a. although
   b. instead
   c. and
   d. but

4. a. but also
   b. whereas
   c. even
   d. rather than

5. a. Instead
   b. But
   c. Rather than
   d. Although

(Exercise 8 is continued on page 24.)

Name _____

Acquiring Knowledge
(continued)

Acquiring scientific knowledge differs somewhat from other forms of learning. Because many scientific discoveries have been made in recent years, old science books may be out of date. These texts may not reflect the findings of modern study and research. For example, a science book published before 1930 will tell you that eight planets revolve around the sun ___6___ there are actually nine. Pluto was not discovered until that year. One way to assess the accuracy of a science book is to check the date of its publication.

Today, most homes contain newspapers and magazines that are filled with information. Some of this information can be believed, ___7___ some of it cannot. One way to assess the credibility of articles in newspapers or magazines is to decide why they were written. Were they written primarily to sell a person, product, or service? If so, the facts and figures they contain may be biased or misleading; ___8___, you would be wise to verify this information by reading articles about these same topics which appear in other publications.

Many people acquire knowledge by listening to the radio or watching television. The accuracy of the information they gain in these ways depends on the research done to prepare it, the sources used, the biases of the writer, ___9___ the viewpoint of the speaker. Because you are seldom aware of the research that others have done or of the biases their work reflects, the best way to check the accuracy of facts you hear on radio and television is to compare them with facts found elsewhere.

Growing up is, in part, a learning process. Children acquire much information between birth and adulthood. ___10___ the learning process does not stop. It continues throughout life. People of all ages need to acquire knowledge, and they need to know how to evaluate the information they are given to determine if it is useful and accurate. If it is not, it should be revised or it should be replaced with new information, ___11___ being passed along to future generations.

6. a. therefore
   b. even though
   c. instead
   d. rather than

7. a. instead
   b. rather than
   c. but
   d. even

8. a. therefore
   b. but
   c. however
   d. and

9. a. however
   b. yet
   c. and
   d. whereas

10. a. Therefore
    b. Whereas
    c. Even though
    d. But

11. a. yet
    b. rather than
    c. but
    d. however

Number of correct answers　_____

Desert Animals

Follow the instructions on page 8. For each numbered line in the passage, choose one of the lettered words or phrases on the right. Underline the word or phrase you choose.

Many interesting and unusual animals inhabit the deserts of California, Arizona, New Mexico, and Texas. Among these animals are elf owls, scorpions, roadrunners, jack rabbits, pack rats, coyotes, and the cactus wren.

Because elf owls are nocturnal—which means that they do their hunting at night—few people ever see them. ___1___, we do know what they look like and where they live. As their name implies, these birds are very small. Usually, they are not more than six inches long. Like other owls, they have hooked beaks and powerful feet with sharp claws, which they use to hold and tear their food. ___2___ building their own homes, elf owls make their nests in abandoned woodpecker holes in giant cacti and Joshua trees.

The scorpion is an arachnid, which means that it is closely related to the spider. Like spiders, scorpions have eight legs. Unlike spiders, scorpions also have a narrow, segmented tail with a poisonous sting at its tip. Normally, scorpions use this weapon to immobilize the small insects and spiders that they eat; ___3___, if scorpions are touched or disturbed, they will sting larger animals or even humans. As a precaution, people who live in the desert often turn their shoes over and tap or shake them before inserting their bare feet. They hope that doing so will dislodge any scorpions that might have crawled inside to take a nap and prevent a nasty sting on the toe.

A curious, somewhat odd-looking bird, the roadrunner gets its name from its habit of darting alongside desert roads in search of food. The roadrunner eats insects, lizards, mice, snails, and snakes. Largely terrestrial, this bird seldom flies. ___4___ it is able to move about on land with surprising speed.

(Exercise 9 is continued on page 26.)

1. a. Instead of
   b. Rather than
   c. Nevertheless
   d. Even though

2. a. And
   b. Instead of
   c. However
   d. Nevertheless

3. a. therefore
   b. even though
   c. instead of
   d. however

4. a. Yet
   b. Instead of
   c. Even though
   d. Therefore

Desert Animals
(continued)

Because of their long ears and large hind legs, jack rabbits can be easily identified as they bound across the desert floor. __5__ these rabbits can go for long periods without drinking water, their bodies do need moisture. They obtain it by nibbling on cactus, a succulent that is able to store water for the long dry spells between desert rains. Jack rabbits often dig burrows under cactus plants, where they can hide from birds of prey, coyotes, and their other natural enemies.

Pack rats are large, bushy-tailed rodents. They are so named because of their curious habit of collecting and hoarding food and miscellaneous objects. These rodents build their nests among the rocks and shrubs. __6__ their nests look like untidy brush piles, pack rats are neater and cleaner than their city cousins.

Coyotes are actually small wolves. Native to western North America, they live in holes in the ground or in caves in rocks. These skillful hunters are helpful because they control the desert population of rodents, such as gophers, mice, rabbits, and rats. __7__, they are also harmful. When these elements of their normal diet are in short supply, they may attack farm and ranch animals.

The cactus wren is the largest wren in the United States. This active, agile bird is extremely useful because it consumes vast quantities of harmful insects. As its name suggests, this wren builts its nest among the seemingly impenetrable thicket of cactus spines and branches; __8__, it comes and goes with relative ease and never gets caught on the needles.

5. a. Although
   b. But
   c. And
   d. However

6. a. But
   b. Therefore
   c. Although
   d. And

7. a. Even though
   b. Nevertheless
   c. Rather than
   d. Therefore

8. a. therefore
   b. although
   c. even though
   d. however

Number of correct answers _____

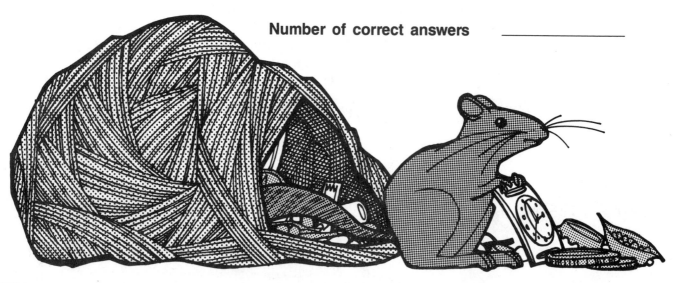

Name _____

Holiday Traditions

Follow the instructions on page 8. For each numbered line in the passage, choose one of the lettered words or phrases on the right. Underline the word or phrase you choose.

Holidays are special days set aside to commemorate significant events. On these days, schools and businesses often close, ___1___ family members gather together to share meals, attend religious services, and tell again the stories that have become part of their holiday traditions.

1. a. and
b. but
c. however
d. even though

The legend of Santa Claus is one of these traditional stories. ___2___ many people think that the idea of Santa is relatively new, it actually originated many years ago in Asia Minor. It is based on the life of St. Nicholas, who was Bishop of Myra during the fourth century. Among other good works, the bishop is said to have put gold in the stockings of the poor; ___3___, in Asia Minor, gifts are exchanged on December 5, St. Nicholas Day Eve, to commemorate his generosity.

2. a. Nevertheless
b. Therefore
c. Instead of
d. Although

3. a. however
b. even though
c. therefore
d. nevertheless

How did Santa Claus become a New World grandfather to whom children whisper their Christmas wishes ___4___ an Old World saint? The American image of Santa Claus was first introduced in a book called *Knickerbocker's History of New York*, which was written by Washington Irving and published in 1809. Knickerbocker's Santa was a Dutchman with baggy breeches, a broad-brimmed hat, ___5___ a magical long pipe. ___6___ filling stockings, this jolly Santa flew over housetops in a wagon, dropping presents down the chimneys of children whose good behavior had earned his favor.

4. a. but
b. instead of
c. and
d. nevertheless

5. a. instead of
b. but
c. and
d. rather than

(Exercise 10 is continued on page 28.)

6. a. Rather than
b. Even though
c. Nevertheless
d. Not only

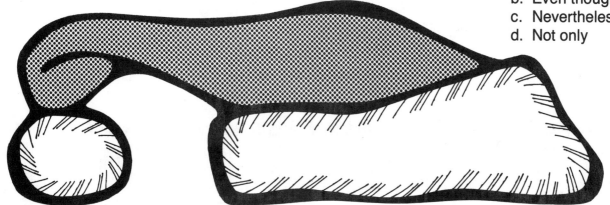

Holiday Traditions
(continued)

Thirteen years later, Clement Clarke Moore wrote a poem entitled "A Visit from St. Nicholas." In this poem, St. Nick is a "jolly old elf" __7__ a dour saint. He rides in a miniature sleigh __8__ a wagon. According to Moore, this sleigh is pulled by a team of eight reindeer, and St. Nick comes down chimneys to fill stockings that have been hung by the fireplace. In Moore's poem, St. Nicholas became Santa Claus, the bearded, grandfatherly figure who personifies the gift-giving spirit of Christmas.

The holiday traditions of Hanukkah are older than St. Nicholas or Christmas. Hanukkah is a celebration of the victory of a relatively few courageous Jewish soldiers over a much larger Syrian army more than two thousand years ago.

As the story goes, a Syrian king named Antiochus had invaded Israel with a large band of soldiers. His goal was to conquer the country and to force its Jewish inhabitants to give up many of their religious customs and beliefs. __9__ agreeing to do so, the Jews resisted. Led by a brave man named Judah Maccabee, they fought for three difficult years. The Syrian army outnumbered the Jewish one, __10__ the Jews were victorious. They drove the invading army out of Israel and once again took control of the Temple of Jerusalem.

The soldiers cleaned and rededicated the temple to the worship of God. In fact, the Hebrew word *Hanukkah* means "rededication." As part of this rededication, they lighted the sacred temple lamp once again. __11__ they had only enough oil to keep the flame burning for one day, it burned for eight. Thus, Hanukkah, the Jewish Feast of Rededication, lasts eight days. When Jewish family members gather during this period, they eat potato pancakes, doughnuts, and other foods that have been cooked in oil. And they light a series of eight candles—one for each night of Hanukkah—as a way of remembering Judah Maccabee's victory and the eight days for which the temple lamp miraculously burned.

7. a. even though
   b. however
   c. and
   d. rather than

8. a. instead of
   b. nevertheless
   c. even though
   d. and

9. a. Nevertheless
   b. Rather than
   c. Even though
   d. However

10. a. and
    b. even though
    c. but
    d. instead of

11. a. Although
    b. Nevertheless
    c. However
    d. And

Number of correct answers _____

Time and Sequence Word Clues

Time is the period during which an action takes place, a process continues, or a condition exists. Time is measurable and has an effect on meaning. Being aware of what a writer is saying about time will help you understand what you read.

Time words are words that tell when, how often, or how many times something happened or will happen. For example, in the sentence below, the word <u>early</u> tells you <u>when</u>, or in what part of the morning, the sun rises.

The sun rises <u>early</u> in the morning.

If you are a careful reader, this piece of information may suggest to you that the season is late spring or summer, when the sun rises early and sets late, rather than late fall or winter, when the sun rises late and sets early. Consider the sentence

The concert pianist practices <u>frequently</u>.

Here, the word <u>frequently</u> indicates <u>how often</u> the pianist practices. Watch for these time words as you read.

after	frequently	occasionally	soon
at last	late	often	then
before	later	repeatedly	usually
early	never	seldom	when
finally	now	sometimes	while

Sequence is order. It is the placement of one thing before or after another. Sequence may be a clue to chronology, relative rank or importance, or cause and effect.

Sequence words are words that indicate the order in which events took place. For example, in the two sentences below, the words *first*, *then*, and *finally* indicate the order in which the three meals of the day—breakfast, lunch, and dinner—are eaten.

During the day, I eat three meals. <u>First</u>, I eat breakfast; <u>then</u>, I eat lunch; and <u>finally</u>, I eat dinner.

Watch for these sequence words as you read.

after	finally	next
as	first	second
before	last	then

Notice where an author uses these words and how they clarify the relative rank or importance of events, describe the order in which these events took place, or suggest the cause-and-effect relationship between them.

Marco Polo

Follow the instructions on page 8. For each numbered line in the passage, choose one of the lettered words or phrases on the right. Underline the word or phrase you choose.

Marco Polo was born ___1___ 1254 in Venice, Italy, a great seaport. His father and uncle traveled from country to country, buying and ___2___ as they went. They were merchants.

In 1271, ___3___ Marco was seventeen years old, he set out with his father and uncle to trade in China, or Cathay, as this ancient country was then known. ___4___, the Polos traveled by ship to the eastern end of the Mediterranean Sea. ___5___, they went by foot and caravan across the varied terrain of Asia. Their amazing journey took them through inhospitable deserts, over cold mountain passes, across seemingly endless plains, and into magnificent cities.

The Polos were away from Venice for about twenty years. When they returned, the rival cities of Venice and Genoa were at war. Captured during a battle, Marco spent nearly a year in prison. ___6___ he was confined, Marco Polo dictated the story of his travels to a fellow prisoner. This man wrote the story in French on parchment by hand. ___7___, the manuscript was translated into more than seventy languages. ___8___, in 1477, it was printed and published as *The Book of Marco Polo*.

Details of Marco Polo's adventures sparked European interest in Far Eastern goods. These goods were very expensive in Europe because of the difficult overland routes by which they had to be imported. Some enterprising merchants speculated that, if the great ocean of which Marco Polo spoke actually existed, then perhaps there was a way to travel to the Far East via an all-water route and a way to bring back its treasured goods so that they would be less costly. Columbus was looking for this sea route to the East when he unexpectedly ran into the American continent.

1. a. when
   b. above
   c. under
   d. around

2. a. stealing
   b. selling
   c. learning
   d. shopping

3. a. when
   b. then
   c. now
   d. finally

4. a. Second
   b. Next
   c. First
   d. At last

5. a. First
   b. At last
   c. Then
   d. Occasionally

6. a. Around
   b. While
   c. First
   d. Next

7. a. Later
   b. Sooner
   c. Early
   d. Before

8. a. First
   b. When
   c. Before
   d. Finally

Number of correct answers _____

Name _____

Vasco da Gama

> Follow the instructions on page 8. For each numbered line in the passage, choose one of the lettered words or phrases on the right. Underline the word or phrase you choose.

In 1492, Columbus tried to reach the fabled riches of the East by sailing west. Five years __1__, in 1497, Vasco da Gama set sail from Lisbon, Portugal, in search of an eastern sea route to India. __2__ sailing down the coast of Africa, through the Cape of Good Hope, and across the Indian Ocean, this Portuguese navigator arrived in May 1498 at Calicut (also called Kozhikode), a port city in southwestern India on the Malabar coast. He and his crew had made the first voyage from western Europe around Africa to the East. His accomplishment was one of the most significant events in Portuguese history.

Opening a sea route to the Eastern world was made even more challenging by several long-held beliefs. __3__, there was the belief that men simply could not live in equatorial heat. Sailing south from Portugal to the tip of Africa meant crossing the equator. __4__, because the coastline of Africa was not well charted, many Europeans mistakenly believed that it was relatively straight and had few inlets. Without inlets, there would be no safe harbors where ships could stop for food and fresh water or take refuge from storms at sea. __5__, sailors feared the doldrums. The doldrums are a part of the ocean near the equator. Calms, squalls, and light shifting winds make sailing in this area frustrating, difficult, and dangerous.

To reach India, Vasco da Gama overcame many obstacles, both real and imagined. __6__ he arrived, he found that his difficulties were not at an end. Overland traders, who had reached India __7__, did not want competition. They turned the Indians against Gama. For a time, the Portuguese navigator could obtain neither the food and supplies he needed for the return trip nor the gold and spices he wanted to take back to prove the success of his voyage. When Vasco da Gama did, __8__, return to Portugal, King Emanuel I rewarded this valiant voyager with the title "Admiral of the Sea of the Indies."

Number of correct answers _____

1. a. earlier
   b. before
   c. later
   d. seldom

2. a. After
   b. Before
   c. When
   d. While

3. a. Second
   b. First
   c. Next
   d. Finally

4. a. First
   b. Finally
   c. Before
   d. Next

5. a. Second
   b. Finally
   c. After
   d. First

6. a. Before
   b. During
   c. When
   d. Soon

7. a. before
   b. early
   c. after
   d. next

8. a. second
   b. when
   c. usually
   d. at last

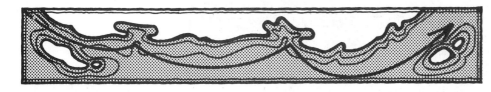

Name _____

Unrecognized Talent

> Follow the instructions on page 8. For each numbered line in the passage, choose one of the lettered words on the right. Underline the word you choose.

Talent often goes unrecognized. __1__, parents and teachers are unaware that it exists. One reason for the failure to identify talent is that people who succeed in __2__ life do not always do well in school. For example, Winston Churchill failed the sixth grade, yet he went on to serve England as prime minister __3__ World War II and to write a six-volume history of that period. Thomas Edison was dismissed by his teachers as being too stupid to learn anything; nevertheless, he became one of the world's most prolific inventors. Even the great English mathematician, Isaac Newton, did poorly in grade school.

If intellectual talent often goes unrecognized, musical talent fares little better. A teacher __4__ told Ludwig van Beethoven that he was hopeless as a composer, yet his Ninth Symphony is an undisputed masterpiece. According to some music critics living __5__, Enrico Caruso is the greatest operatic tenor who ever lived; but, __6__ this tenor's lifetime, a teacher told him that he had no voice and could not sing.

Employers seem to be no better than teachers at spotting talent. For example, a newspaper editor fired Walt Disney because he lacked ideas. __7__, the "unimaginative" Disney created the first feature-length animated films and designed Disneyland. Another editor told Louisa May Alcott that she would never write anything with popular appeal. Yet the invincible woman __8__ authored a highly successful series of books based on her family's experiences.

Talent often goes unrecognized—perhaps because we do not know where to look or because, in looking for it, we overlook the very things we are looking for.

1. a. Finally
   b. Frequently
   c. Seldom
   d. Never

2. a. later
   b. earlier
   c. early
   d. after

3. a. early
   b. late
   c. during
   d. often

4. a. once
   b. finally
   c. seldom
   d. then

5. a. then
   b. before
   c. often
   d. now

6. a. during
   b. when
   c. before
   d. after

7. a. Before
   b. Earlier
   c. Later
   d. When

8. a. then
   b. earlier
   c. before
   d. now

Number of correct answers _____

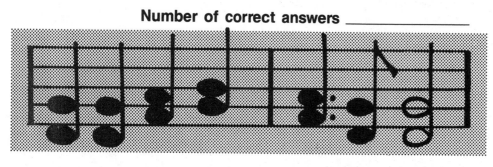

Painting with Colored Chalk

> Follow the instructions on page 8. For each numbered line in the passage, choose one of the lettered words on the right. Underline the word you choose.

To paint a picture with colored chalk, first gather together all of the materials you will need—several sheets of newspaper, a piece of manila drawing paper, some liquid starch (mixed so that it is thin, but not runny), and some colored chalk. ___1___, follow these instructions carefully.

First, select a clean, flat, smooth work surface and lay your newspapers on it. ___2___, fasten the manila paper securely to the newspaper by putting a small amount of starch under each of the four corners of the manila paper and gently smoothing it against the newspaper with your hands.

Third, coat the entire surface of the manila paper evenly with starch. ___3___, divide this surface into three horizontal parts by running your index finger across the starch in two places. Let the top part be the sky, the middle part be distant hills or mountains, and the bottom part be the nearer ground.

___4___, select one of these parts and blend the colored chalks into it. As you work, remember that distant colors are usually paler than close ones. To achieve this effect in your picture, put smaller amounts of color on the distant areas.

___5___, leave the painting to dry. While it is drying, think about how you intend to finish it. ___6___, when the background colors have dried, add details. As you do so, remember that small or intricate details are not visible at a distance. If you add objects to the more distant parts of your picture, do not paint them in minute detail.

___7___ you have finished adding detail, again leave the painting to dry. ___8___ your chalk painting is completely dry, share it with other members of your class by posting it on a bulletin board or wall.

Number of correct answers _____

1. a. Before
   b. Then
   c. After
   d. Finally

2. a. Second
   b. First
   c. Finally
   d. Now

3. a. Second
   b. Third
   c. Fourth
   d. Last

4. a. First
   b. Third
   c. Last
   d. Next

5. a. When
   b. Then
   c. Third
   d. Finally

6. a. First
   b. Next
   c. Finally
   d. Fourth

7. a. After
   b. Before
   c. Early
   d. Late

8. a. When
   b. Before
   c. Finally
   d. Then

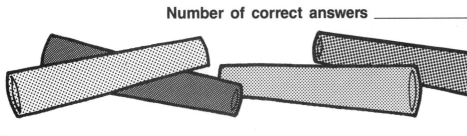

Living in Space

Follow the instructions on page 8. For each numbered line in the passage, choose one of the lettered words on the right. Underline the word you choose.

Would you like to become a crew member on the space shuttle? __1__ you say yes, you should be aware that the space environment is extremely inhospitable. Temperatures can vary from 250° F in the sun to −150° F in the shade. In addition, there are cosmic rays, solar flares, and other harmful forms of radiation. To this list you can add such other __2__ as micrometeoroids.

Because the hazards of space were considered __3__ the shuttle was being designed, crew members can live aboard in relative safety and comfort. Before crew members could live in space, however, shuttle designers had to find a way to maintain a healthful environment within the crew compartment. __4__, they had to supply oxygen for crew members to breathe when they inhaled. __5__, they had to find a safe way to eliminate the carbon dioxide which built up as crew members exhaled.

Another design problem was gravity and the way shuttle crew members experienced its pull. __6__ ascent, they felt the sensation of increased weight. Once they had reached orbit, they felt a lack of weight. Because of this __7__, all items used in the crew compartment had to be anchored with magnets or contained to keep them from floating free.

(Exercise 15 is continued on page 35.)

1. a. After
   b. Before
   c. When
   d. During

2. a. temperatures
   b. flares
   c. radiation
   d. hazards

3. a. while
   b. before
   c. after
   d. during

4. a. Next
   b. Last
   c. Second
   d. First

5. a. Then
   b. When
   c. First
   d. Now

6. a. While
   b. During
   c. When
   d. Before

7. a. "mass"
   b. "gravity"
   c. "hazard"
   d. "weightlessness"

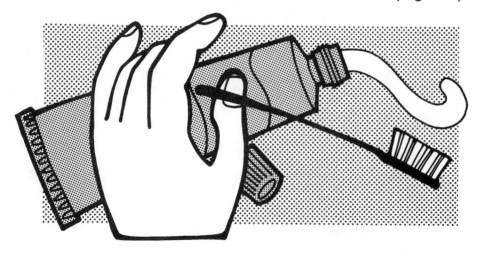

Living in Space
(continued)

Designers could not solve all of the problems, and crew members must make many adjustments. For example, __8__ going into space, shuttle crew members must learn new ways of doing everyday things. Weightlessness in space makes it impossible to eat, drink, and __9__ in exactly the same ways one would on earth.

Shuttle crew members must learn how to prepare and eat meals in space. Meals aboard __10__ space flights consisted only of foods that could be compressed into bite-sized tablets or pureed and packaged in squeezable metal tubes. Because these meals lacked variety, eating them was boring. Menus aboard __11__ space flights have been a distinct improvement. Among the fresh, dehydrated, and freeze-dried entrées shuttle crew members eat are sliced beef, ham, and turkey with gravy. Many other foods—including nuts, granola bars, and even Life Savers—are carried aboard.

Sleeping accommodations aboard the shuttle are also very different from those on __12__. Within the crew compartment are three horizontal bunks and one vertical bunk. Because of weightlessness, there is really no up or down in space. In fact, the shuttle's bottom horizontal bunk faces the floor!

Becoming a crew member aboard the shuttle may sound exciting, but not everyone can adjust to life in space—even for a relatively short period of time.

8. a. after
   b. while
   c. before
   d. when

9. a. swallow
   b. sleep
   c. dine
   d. type

10. a. late
    b. later
    c. fast
    d. early

11. a. later
    b. early
    c. earlier
    d. slow

12. a. board
    b. space
    c. earth
    d. shuttle

Number of correct answers _____

Humphrey, the Wrong-Way Whale

> Follow the instructions on page 8. For each numbered line in the passage, choose one of the lettered words on the right. Underline the word you choose.

During the fall months, humpback whales swim south along the Pacific shoreline toward warmer waters. __1__ spring comes, they move north toward their summer home in colder waters. One year, __2__ this seasonal migration, an unfortunate humpback made a wrong turn into Oakland Harbor and __3__ swam up the Sacramento River.

Having gone upriver, the hapless humpback got stuck in a dead-end channel called Shag Slough. Humphrey, as the media christened the enormous mammal, sat in this narrow channel for nearly a week. He was unable to swim forward and unwilling to turn around and head back out to sea.

Scientists and animal lovers came to California from all over the country to try to help the whale. They tried first one thing and __4__ another. __5__, they found that playing loud percussion music underwater caused the leviathan to turn around and begin to swim back downriver.

But the problem was not solved. __6__ Humphrey swam through the first set of bridges, he stopped and would go no farther. People __7__ tried herding the whale with noise, but this time he would not respond.

Consulted experts and concerned bystanders made many suggestions. Some wanted to lift the confused whale by crane and carry him to safety. Others wanted to throw a large net over Humphrey and tow him out to sea. __8__, someone decided to broadcast the sounds of migrating humpback whales from his boat. On hearing these familiar sounds, Humphrey began to follow the boat. In fact, he chased it more than fifty miles, back to San Francisco Bay and the safety of the Pacific Ocean.

Number of correct answers _____

1. a. During
   b. Later
   c. When
   d. Earlier

2. a. while
   b. during
   c. after
   d. before

3. a. now
   b. first
   c. before
   d. then

4. a. then
   b. first
   c. last
   d. third

5. a. During
   b. Then
   c. Finally
   d. Before

6. a. During
   b. After
   c. Again
   d. Then

7. a. still
   b. when
   c. again
   d. now

8. a. First
   b. Next
   c. When
   d. Finally

Summary and Concluding Word Clues

so · for this reason · in summary · thus

to summarize · briefly · in conclusion

A **summary** is a brief statement of the main points that have been made. A **conclusion** is a reasoned judgment based on the facts that have been presented. A careful author often writes a summary paragraph at the end of his article. If the article is long, he may also write a summary sentence at the end of each paragraph or section. If the author has presented an argument or the purpose of his article is to persuade readers to share his opinion or to adopt a particular point of view, he may list his conclusions in addition to, or instead of, writing a summary.

Summary and concluding words are words and phrases that introduce a summary or a conclusion. These words should alert you to read carefully because they usually come before the facts or ideas an author believes to be most important. For example, look at these three sentences.

> Scale insects destroy citrus trees. Ladybugs
> eat scale insects. <u>Consequently</u>, ladybugs are
> very important to California citrus growers.

In the first sentence, the author presents a fact about the relationship between scale insects and citrus trees. In the second sentence, the author presents a fact about the relationship between ladybugs and scale insects. In the third sentence, the author draws a conclusion about the relationship between ladybugs and citrus growers based on the facts he has presented in these first two sentences. The word <u>Consequently</u> tells you that this conclusion is coming and should alert you to read more carefully so that you will *not* miss the point!

Watch for these summary and concluding words as you read.

as a result	in summary
briefly	so
consequently	therefore
for this reason	thus
hence	to summarize
in conclusion	to sum up

When you see these words and phrases, note especially what the author has written *after* them.

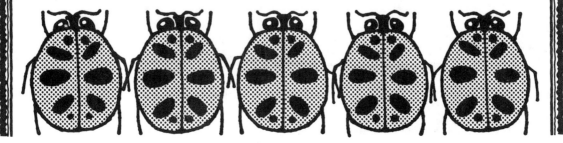

Name _____

A Different Kind of Tea Party

> Follow the instructions on page 8. For each numbered line in the passage, choose one of the lettered words or phrases on the right. Underline the word or phrase you choose.

During the first half of the eighteenth century, the American colonies belonged to England. England used her __1__ to make money. She got raw materials from them, and she sold manufactured goods to them.

Because the American colonies belonged to England, the English king and parliament made laws to govern them. Some of these __2__ taxed the colonists. The colonists did not like being forced to pay __3__ when they were not allowed to help make the laws.

The colonists were especially unhappy about an import tax on tea. In some colonial cities, when British ships carrying tea arrived, agents refused to receive the tea, and the ships were forced to turn around and return to England without unloading. In other __4__, the unwanted tea was stored in government warehouses because there was no one on hand to pay the tax.

In the winter of 1773, when a British ship carrying tea steamed into Boston Harbor, the citizens of Boston voted that the ship should not be permitted to dock and unload. Instead, they demanded that it return to England with its unwanted cargo. The ship's officers refused. That night, a band of __5__ disguised themselves as Indians. They boarded the British ship as it lay at anchor and __6__ boxes of tea overboard.

__7__, the colonists felt frustrated by British taxation policies. They protested by throwing boxes of British tea into Boston Harbor. This event has since become known as the Boston Tea Party.

1. a. century
   b. country
   c. colonies
   d. imports

2. a. English
   b. colonies
   c. laws
   d. years

3. a. Americans
   b. taxes
   c. colonies
   d. laws

4. a. cities
   b. ships
   c. agents
   d. taxes

5. a. Indians
   b. agents
   c. colonists
   d. officers

6. a. sailed
   b. broke
   c. drank
   d. threw

7. a. Therefore
   b. When
   c. In summary
   d. First

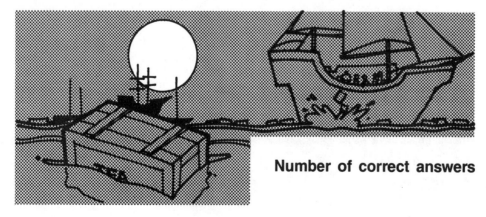

Number of correct answers _____

How a Tree Obtains Food

Follow the instructions on page 8. For each numbered line in the passage, choose one of the lettered words on the right. Underline the word you choose.

Animals must move about to look for food. Trees cannot move around. They are rooted in one place. Trees must make __1__ using the air, water, and sunlight that come their way.

A tree takes water from the soil through its roots. This __2__ and the nutrients it contains go up the trunk, out the branches, and into the leaves of the tree. Air enters these leaves through tiny holes in their surfaces called pores.

The __3__ contain chlorophyll, an important enzyme. This __4__ gives tree leaves their green color. It also enables them to act as tiny laboratories in which __5__ from the sun is used in chemical reactions which change air and water into compounds the tree can use as food. This process in which plants use light to make food is called **photosynthesis**.

__6__, because a tree cannot move about in search of food, it must make its own. This food is made in the leaves during a process known as photosynthesis. When sunlight is present, an enzyme called chlorophyll enables the tree to use air and water to make food.

1. a. water
   b. shade
   c. air
   d. food

2. a. roots
   b. water
   c. soil
   d. shade

3. a. roots
   b. trees
   c. leaves
   d. pores

4. a. enzyme
   b. leaves
   c. soil
   d. pores

5. a. flares
   b. light
   c. food
   d. enzyme

6. a. First
   b. Next
   c. Briefly
   d. Then

Number of correct answers _____

Corn

Follow the instructions on page 8. For each numbered line in the passage, choose one of the lettered words or phrases on the right. Underline the word or phrase you choose.

Corn is an ancient food. It originated seven thousand years ago when Indian farmers first tamed a wild variety of this ___1___ crop and began to cultivate it in the highland valleys of central and northeastern Mexico.

Ancient corn did not look much like the ___2___ variety we buy in supermarkets. The full-grown cobs were not even as large as your little finger. But careful cultivation during the next 4,500 years produced ___3___ almost half the size of those we eat today.

As a crop, corn proved to be remarkably adaptable. It could be grown at elevations ranging from sea level to 12,000 feet. This unusual ___4___ range meant that corn could be cultivated throughout Central and South America. It sooned joined beans and squash as staples of the Mesoamerican diet.

As a food, corn was quite versatile. It could be used as both a vegetable and a grain. The kernels could be cooked and eaten or they could be dried and ground into a meal. This ___5___ could, in turn, be used to make both tortillas and cornbread.

From its humble beginnings in the highland valleys of Mexico, corn spread throughout the world. Portuguese and Spanish explorers carried seed corn back to Europe. Other ___6___ carried corn from Mexico to the Philippines. From there, it was taken to other Asiatic islands and to China. In time, corn was grown along the eastern and western coasts of Africa.

Corn also spread north. Today, it is the most important cereal crop in the Western Hemisphere. It is grown in every state in the Union. The size of the annual corn crop is much greater than that of any other grain crop. Surprisingly, an acre of ___7___ has more food value than an acre of any other grain crop!

Corn adapts well and feeds many. ___8___, hungry people all over the globe owe a debt of gratitude to the ancient farmers in Mexico who first cultivated it.

Number of correct answers _____

1. a. fruit
   b. cereal
   c. dairy
   d. tropical

2. a. canned
   b. early
   c. modern
   d. fresh

3. a. ears
   b. leaves
   c. stalks
   d. stems

4. a. mountain
   b. size
   c. weight
   d. climatic

5. a. kernel
   b. corn
   c. meal
   d. vegetable

6. a. explorers
   b. Portuguese
   c. Spanish
   d. farmers

7. a. oats
   b. corn
   c. wheat
   d. barley

8. a. Briefly
   b. However
   c. Because
   d. For these reasons

Drinking Water

> Follow the instructions on page 8. For each numbered line in the passage, choose one of the lettered words on the right. Underline the word you choose.

All communities, regardless of their size or location, must find ways of providing an adequate supply of pure, safe drinking water for their residents.

Different communities get their ___1___ water from different sources. For example, some communities get their ___2___ from nearby lakes and streams. Other communities pump their water from underground wells. Still other ___3___ ensure that they will have enough water by building dams and creating reservoirs to catch and store the water that falls to earth as rain or snow. And still other communities import their water from ___4___ regions by means of special pipes or troughs called **aquaducts**.

No matter where community drinking water comes from, it must be tested to make certain that it is ___5___. As water moves through the ground or across the land, it may become contaminated. Fertilizers, pesticides, petroleum products, sewage, and other harmful substances may flow or fall into it. Before ___6___ water can be drunk, it must be purified.

Sometimes drinking water must also be treated to improve the taste or adjust the hardness. "Hardness" may not be a quality you associate with water, but hard water is water that contains large amounts of dissolved salts, such as calcium or magnesium. ___7___ water is difficult to use for bathing or washing because these ___8___ prevent soap from sudsing and will not allow dirt to be easily dissolved or rinsed away. Often the minerals that make water hard also give it an unpleasant taste. For these reasons, water intended for drinking or home use is usually treated to soften it and to improve its taste.

In conclusion, although communities get their drinking water from a variety of sources, most of them must test and treat it to ensure that it is pure, not too hard, and does not have an unpleasant taste.

Number of correct answers _____

1. a. running
   b. washing
   c. irrigation
   d. drinking

2. a. water
   b. food
   c. weather
   d. drinking

3. a. states
   b. communities
   c. farms
   d. countries

4. a. higher
   b. drier
   c. wetter
   d. richer

5. a. hard
   b. wet
   c. safe
   d. soft

6. a. drinking
   b. hard
   c. soft
   d. contaminated

7. a. Hard
   b. Soft
   c. Well
   d. Rain

8. a. tastes
   b. salts
   c. amounts
   d. suds

Forests and Furs, Forts and Outposts

Follow the instructions on page 8. For each numbered line in the passage, choose one of the lettered words or phrases on the right. Underline the word or phrase you choose.

By 1750, many of the forests in the Old World had disappeared. For centuries, European villagers had been clearing the land for farms and using the wood for fuel, furniture, and shelter. In many places, there were few ___1___ among which fur-bearing animals could hunt and hide. As a result, parts of Europe were home to relatively few of these ___2___—certainly not enough to meet the growing European demand for coats, hats, blankets, rugs, and other items of apparel and decoration.

At the same time in the New World, the forests stood thick and untouched. The Indians living in these ___3___ gathered fallen branches but were little inclined to clear large areas. Before the white men came, these ___4___ hunted only the animals whose flesh they needed for food or whose hides they wanted for clothing or shelter but seldom killed for sport or profit.

The French explorers, who were among the first white men to see the interior of North America, recognized that much of the wealth of this new land lay in its abundant and untapped resources—its fertile land, its forests, and its fur-bearing animals. Instead of searching for gold, as the Spaniards had done in Central and South America, these explorers traded for ___5___.

These eager French traders built forts near Indian villages to facilitate trading and to protect their interests. ___6___, many cities in what are now Canada and the United States actually began as fur-trading outposts, where white men came to get supplies and Indians came to exchange their pelts for the white man's blankets, beads, bullets, guns, and tools. These ___7___, which were originally established to aid the fur trade, later became way stations for settlers moving west.

1. a. houses
   b. trees
   c. farms
   d. rocks

2. a. forests
   b. trees
   c. animals
   d. Indians

3. a. meadows
   b. deserts
   c. mountains
   d. woodlands

4. a. Indians
   b. traders
   c. trappers
   d. Frenchmen

5. a. guns
   b. beads
   c. tools
   d. furs

6. a. First
   b. Consequently
   c. Finally
   d. Then

7. a. forts
   b. way stations
   c. outposts
   d. cities

Number of correct answers _____

Name _____

The Formation of the American Continents

Follow the instructions on page 8. For each numbered line in the passage, choose one of the lettered words on the right. Underline the word you choose.

Millions of years ago, the earth was an intensely hot sphere. Clouds of steam rose from it, forming a blanket of ___1___ that enveloped it completely.

As the ___2___ cooled, it got smaller. These contractions caused its crust to fold and wrinkle, thus forming both high places and low ones. At the same time, the vapor in the clouds condensed into drops, which fell on the earth as rain, covering its surface with ___3___. While the low places lay beneath this water as ocean floor, some of the high places were thrust up even farther and became the land masses we call islands and continents.

Although the American continents are often called the New World, they are really an ___4___ world. Part of the North American continent stood above sea level when all of the other ___5___, except two regions in northern Europe, were still under water.

The oldest land in North America is a group of mountains that lie north of the Great Lakes in Canada. Alternate exposure to extremes of heat and cold caused these ancient mountains to crack. Waves beating incessantly upon them eventually broke free huge pieces of rock. Rubbed and knocked together by the sea, these ___6___ were gradually broken into smaller rocks, then into pebbles, and finally, into particles, which were deposited at the base of the mountains as soil.

(Exercise 22 is continued on page 44.)

1. a. vapor
   b. dust
   c. pollution
   d. smog

2. a. vapor
   b. earth
   c. steam
   d. blanket

3. a. air
   b. vapor
   c. crust
   d. water

4. a. energetic
   b. wet
   c. old
   d. new

5. a. islands
   b. mountains
   c. folds
   d. continents

6. a. boulders
   b. pebbles
   c. sands
   d. cracks

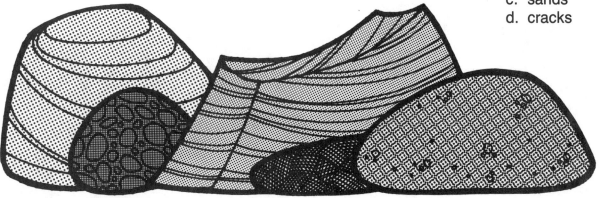

Name _____

The Formation of the American Continents
(continued)

As time went on, more folds in the earth's surface were lifted above the water. These ___7___ became the Green Mountains and the White Mountains of New England, the Adirondack Mountains of New York, and the Blue Ridge Mountains, which extend from Pennsylvania south as far as northern Georgia.

Ages passed. Far out on the west coast, the earth's crust shrank and wrinkled again. Hundreds of miles of rock layers were squeezed together and thrust up to form ranges of mountains that extend from the Arctic Ocean to the tip of South America. We know these ___8___ as the Rockies, the Cascades, the Sierra Nevada, the Sierra Madre, and the Andes.

The flat area between the eastern and western mountains lay for a long time beneath the sea. It was thrust up by further movements of the earth's restless ___9___. And it was filled in by ___10___ that was washed down from the surrounding peaks.

The great forces of nature that began to form the American continents millions of years ago are still at work ___11___. Earthquakes lift and lower portions of the earth's crust. Volcanoes create mountain cones. Glaciers carve deep gorges. Rivers widen the valleys through which they flow and move soil from their sources to their mouths. Storms batter the land and alter the seacoasts forever. Thus, the ___12___ of the American continents remains the unfinished business of the forces of nature.

7. a. folds
   b. mountains
   c. ranges
   d. states

8. a. wrinkles
   b. miles
   c. mountains
   d. layers

9. a. miles
   b. crust
   c. continents
   d. mountains

10. a. snow
    b. water
    c. crust
    d. soil

11. a. then
    b. today
    c. yesterday
    d. ago

12. a. formation
    b. destruction
    c. disruption
    d. eruption

Number of correct answers _____

Score Chart

Exercise Number	Page Numbers	Number of Answers Needed	Number of Correct Answers	Percent Score
Noun Substitute Clues				
1	10–11	8		
2	12–13	12		
3	14–15	12		
4	16–17	12		
5	18	8		
Transforming Word Clues				
6	20–21	7		
7	22	6		
8	23–24	11		
9	25–26	8		
10	27–28	11		
Time and Sequence Word Clues				
11	30	8		
12	31	8		
13	32	8		
14	33	8		
15	34–35	12		
16	36	8		
Summary Word Clues				
17	38	7		
18	39	6		
19	40	8		
20	41	8		
21	42	7		
22	43–44	12		

Table of Percentages

Number of Answers Needed	Number of Correct Answers Supplied													
	1	2	3	4	5	6	7	8	9	10	11	12	13	14
1	100													
2	50	100												
3	33	67	100											
4	25	50	75	100										
5	20	40	60	80	100									
6	17	33	50	67	83	100								
7	14	29	43	57	71	86	100							
8	13	25	38	50	63	75	88	100						
9	11	22	33	44	56	67	78	89	100					
10	10	20	30	40	50	60	70	80	90	100				
11	9	18	27	36	45	55	64	73	82	91	100			
12	8	17	25	33	42	50	58	67	75	83	92	100		
13	8	15	23	31	38	46	54	62	69	77	85	92	100	
14	7	14	21	29	36	43	50	57	64	71	79	86	93	100

****

Answer Key

Exercise 1, Pages 10–11
Interesting Animals That Live Around Us
1. b. lizard
2. c. rodent
3. d. their
4. c. birds
5. c. bird
6. b. it
7. a. Their
8. c. beetles

Exercise 2, Pages 12–13
How Living Things Swim
1. c. creatures
2. b. they
3. c. They
4. c. their
5. d. creature
6. c. its
7. b. its
8. d. itself
9. a. it
10. c. its
11. d. Their
12. d. creatures

Exercise 3, Pages 14–15
Smokey Bear, the Famous Forest Ranger
1. c. his
2. c. him
3. d. his
4. b. He
5. c. cub
6. b. bear
7. d. house
8. b. it
9. c. it
10. c. them
11. b. adults
12. b. their

Exercise 4, Pages 16–17
A Different Kind of Home
1. c. insect
2. b. their
3. c. insect
4. d. their
5. d. grass-dweller
6. d. their
7. c. creatures
8. a. worms
9. a. her
10. b. young
11. c. city
12. b. These

Exercise 5, Page 18
Central America
1. b. nations
2. a. they
3. c. area
4. d. groups
5. c. explorer
6. a. natives
7. b. He
8. d. treasure

Exercise 6, Pages 20–21
Sleepwalking
1. c. however
2. a. but
3. b. but
4. c. Nevertheless
5. d. but
6. a. Rather than
7. d. however

Exercise 7, Page 22
Changing Times
1. c. however
2. b. whereas
3. a. Although
4. b. On the other hand
5. d. even though
6. c. but

Exercise 8, Pages 23–24
Acquiring Knowledge
1. b. Although
2. d. Instead
3. c. and
4. a. but also
5. d. Although
6. b. even though
7. c. but
8. a. therefore
9. c. and
10. d. But
11. b. rather than

Exercise 9, Pages 25–26
Desert Animals
1. c. Nevertheless
2. b. Instead of
3. d. however
4. a. Yet
5. a. Although
6. c. Although
7. b. Nevertheless
8. d. however

Exercise 10, Pages 27–28
Holiday Traditions
1. a. and
2. d. Although
3. c. therefore
4. b. instead of
5. c. and
6. a. Rather than
7. d. rather than
8. a. instead of
9. b. Rather than
10. c. but
11. a. Although

Exercise 11, Page 30
Marco Polo
1. d. around
2. b. selling
3. a. when
4. c. First
5. c. Then
6. b. While
7. a. Later
8. d. Finally

Answer Key
(continued)

Exercise 12, Page 31
Vasco da Gama
1. c. later
2. a. After
3. b. First
4. d. Next
5. b. Finally
6. c. When
7. a. before
8. d. at last

Exercise 13, Page 32
Unrecognized Talent
1. b. Frequently
2. a. later
3. c. during
4. a. once
5. d. now
6. a. during
7. c. Later
8. a. then

Exercise 14, Page 33
Painting with Colored Chalk
1. b. Then
2. a. Second
3. c. Fourth
4. d. Next
5. b. Then
6. c. Finally
7. a. After
8. a. When

Exercise 15, Pages 34–35
Living in Space
1. b. Before
2. d. hazards
3. a. while
4. d. First
5. a. Then
6. b. During
7. d. "weightlessness"
8. c. before
9. b. sleep
10. d. early
11. a. later
12. c. earth

Exercise 16, Page 36
Humphrey, the Wrong-Way Whale
1. c. When
2. b. during
3. d. then
4. a. then
5. c. Finally
6. b. After
7. c. again
8. d. Finally

Exercise 17, Page 38
A Different Kind of Tea Party
1. c. colonies
2. c. laws
3. b. taxes
4. a. cities
5. c. colonists
6. d. threw
7. c. In summary

Exercise 18, Page 39
How a Tree Obtains Food
1. d. food
2. b. water
3. c. leaves
4. a. enzyme
5. b. light
6. c. Briefly

Exercise 19, Page 40
Corn
1. b. cereal
2. c. modern
3. a. ears
4. d. climatic
5. c. meal
6. a. explorers
7. b. corn
8. d. For these reasons

Exercise 20, Page 41
Drinking Water
1. d. drinking
2. a. water
3. b. communities
4. c. wetter
5. c. safe
6. d. contaminated
7. a. Hard
8. b. salts

Exercise 21, Page 42
Forests and Furs, Forts and Outposts
1. b. trees
2. c. animals
3. d. woodlands
4. a. Indians
5. d. furs
6. b. Consequently
7. c. outposts

Exercise 22, Pages 43–44
The Formation of the American Continents
1. a. vapor
2. b. earth
3. d. water
4. c. old
5. d. continents
6. a. boulders
7. a. folds
8. c. mountains
9. b. crust
10. d. soil
11. b. today
12. a. formation

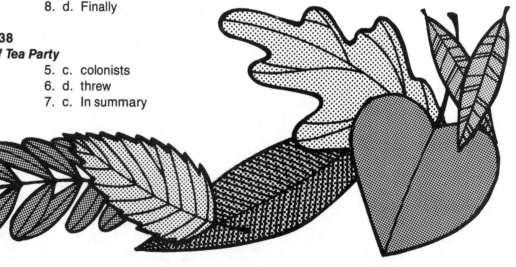